This Book Belongs To

Made in the USA
Las Vegas, NV
13 July 2023

74707065R00061